THE NIGHT AFTER CHRISTMAS

Kes Gray and Claire Powell

To Julie (and your Christmas Rocky Road!) - KG
To Cressida, Cressmas forever - CP

HODDER CHILDREN'S BOOKS
First published in Great Britain in 2020 by Hodder and Stoughton

A CIP catalogue record for this book is available from the British Library.

HB ISBN: 9781 444 95465 4
PB ISBN: 9781 444 95466 1

1 3 5 7 9 10 8 6 4 2

Printed and bound in China

Hodder Children's Books
An imprint of Hachette Children's Group
Part of Hodder and Stoughton
Carmelite House
50 Victoria Embankment
London, EC4Y 0DZ

An Hachette UK Company
www.hachette.co.uk
www.hachettechildrens.co.uk

FSC
www.fsc.org
MIX
Paper from responsible sources
FSC® C104740

THE NIGHT AFTER CHRISTMAS

Kes Gray and Claire Powell

Hodder Children's Books

'Twas the night after Christmas (that's late Boxing Day),
And Santa was putting his toy sack away.

The sleigh had been covered, mileage recorded,
Presents delivered, reindeer rewarded.

With magic sack now under gold lock and key,
Santa sat down for his welcome-home tea.

"A toast!" declared Santa, raising his glass.
"To Christmases future and Christmases past!"

Elves dressed in festive onesies and jumpers
Were gathered outside in rather large numbers.

Another year over, a Christmas job done.
Excitement was growing. It was time for some fun!

It was time for the moment that elves love the most:
The Boxing-night party. But where was their host?

"SANTA!" they shouted,
"Owl Time is nigh!"

Santa stepped out and looked to the sky.

"On Snowy! On Ghost! On Blizzard! On Snowball!
On Milkshake, on Whitefly. On Misty and Noble!"

Swifter than peregrines, eight giant owls flew,
Propelled by the sound of Santa's who's-who.
They carried a cracker the size of a bus.
It was huge. It was vast. It was XXL-plus.
Jam-packed with goodies, bulgingly full,
It was crammed. It was rammed. It was ready to pull . . .

"Christmas," said Santa, "is a time to BELIEVE!
Get ready, get steady, make a wish and NOW HEAVE!"

The elves dug their heels in,
wrestled and quivered . . .

the cracker EXPLODED and duly delivered.

Whistles and flutes rained down from the sky.
Jelly beans, lollipops (and the occasional mince pie).

Cracker smoke spiralled, magic dust plumed,
Glitter cascaded, zizzywigs zoomed.

As the elves tumbled backwards in sixes and sevens,
Mrs Claus pulled a lever and switched on the heavens.

Pinks turned to purple, greens turned to red.
A Boxing-night light show blazed overhead.

Twinkle by twinkle, stars moved to new stations,
Lacing the sky with Yule constellations.

The Snowflake, The Sugar Cane, The Church Bell, The Trumpet.
The Snowman, The Angel, The Hot Buttered Crumpet.

Santa hurrahed and pulled up his boots
as the party erupted with rooty-toot-toots!

There were dance-offs to enter and prizes to win.
Even the reindeer came and joined in.

Dasher and Dancer
did the fandango.

Donner and Blitzen
tackled the tango.

Comet and Cupid
were tops at the twist,

Prancer's moonwalk
was not to be missed.

Everyone partied
and busted their moves.
Apart from poor Vixen
(she has four left hooves).

The Boxing-night party went right through the night,
On until dawn and through to first light.

As the stars took a bow and the northern lights faded,
Santa yawned loudly. He felt rather jaded.

With a clap of his hands and a blast of a whistle
the party dispersed like the down of a thistle.

Elves in pyjamas took to their beds.

Reindeer lay down
and rested their heads.

With a mistletoe kiss and a whispered "sleep tight"
a jolly old couple retired for the night.
In the blink of an eye they had started to snore.
Sleeps until Christmas?

Just three sixty-four!